Dr. Dee Dee Dynamo's
Meteorite Mission

By Oneeka Williams M.D.
Illustrated by Valerie Bouthyette

Dr. Dee Dee Dynamo's Meteorite Mission

PRT1113A

Library of Congress Control Number: 2013952273

Printed in the United States
ISBN-13: 9781620865545
ISBN-10: 1620865548
www.mascotbooks.com

Wooshhhhhhhhhhhhhhhh!

Dr. Dee Dee Dynamo, girl super surgeon, zips through her bedroom window into the cool, refreshing morning air. The sun is rising over the placid waters surrounding the Island of Positivity and Dr. Dee Dee is CHARGED UP and READY to go.

She zooms over to her best friend and cousin Lukas' house and waves at his dad and little brother, Jakey.

"Good morning, Uncle Huebs. Where is Lukas?"

"He's still asleep!" responds Uncle Huebs.

Seconds later, Dr. Dee Dee reaches through Lukas' bedroom window and nudges him.

"Wake up, sleepyhead," she teases. Then, in a flash, she whisks back home.

2

Dr. Dee Dee Dynamo lives in Battery Grove with her parents and grandparents. Mommy and Daddy Dynamo knew from an early age that Dr. Dee Dee had special abilities. Her hands glowed when she was born! And when Dr. Dee Dee was only three months old, Mommy Dynamo found her at the top of their mango tree, repairing a baby bird's wing.

Granddad Willy has just collected baskets of fruit from the garden. "Good morning, dearie. We are going to have a picnic-style breakfast."

"Oh boy, Granddad Willy! I can't wait to taste what Grandma B has prepared!" Dr. Dee Dee says.

Grandma B chuckles. "Dee Dee, I know you have lots of electrical energy but my breakfast will add some pep to your step!"

"Good morning, Dee Dee," greets Mommy Dynamo. "After breakfast, you will do your schoolwork and review your mission to Pluto. My sixth-grade science class completed their module on dwarf planets and would love you to come visit and share your experience."

"Awesome!" replies Dr. Dee Dee.

Gordon the Gullible Globe chimes in. "I heard Pluto telling his moon, Charon, that he was very happy when Dr. Dee Dee operated on him. He said all he felt was a little pinch."

Kyle the Koala Bear, who is munching on his eucalyptus leaves, gives a skeptical look and grumbles, "I am still irritated with Pluto. In my opinion, that mission to restore Pluto to a planet was a complete waste of time."

"Oh well," he yawns. "I must catch up on my rest."

"Oh Kyle, despite your complaints, I know you love being my assistant!" laughs Dr. Dee Dee. "Let's take Ana Anesthetic and Sydnee Syringe on future missions so that our patients won't feel even the slightest pinch."

"Psssst! Psssssssssssssst!"

Dr. Dee Dee looks behind her and sees Lukas hiding on the other side of the fence trying his utmost to catch her attention.

"I see you, Lukas," says Mommy Dynamo. "You also need to get your notebook and review what you learned about Pluto!"

"Awwwww, maaan!" complains Lukas.

WAHOO! WAHOO! WAHOO!

It's Gordon the Gullible Globe, screeching loudly, spinning frantically, and flashing his blue lights. That can only mean one thing. Somewhere in the universe, someone needs Dr. Dee Dee Dynamo's help!

"Yippee!" Lukas grins. "Saved by the globe!"

Kyle startles from his nap and groans, "Really? Now what?"

"What is it, Gordon?" Dr. Dee Dee asks.

"Astrid Asteroid is wailing because a part of her has broken off and she doesn't know where it went," says Gordon. "Then I heard a loud BOOM that came from Earth's Northern Hemisphere."

"What happened?" asks Lukas.

"A meteor has crashed into Earth," Gordon responds.

"If it has crashed into Earth then it is called a meteorite," announces Kyle haughtily.

"Well, *excuuuuuse* me," replies Gordon in a miffed tone.

"Holymackarolee!" exclaims Lukas. "Where in the world did the meteorite come from?"

"I guess we have found Astrid's missing piece," grunts Kyle sarcastically.

Dr. Dee Dee explains. "Most meteorites are pieces of rock that break off from asteroids located between the orbits of Mars and Jupiter. Other times asteroids and comets collide with Mars or Earth's moon causing small rocks to break off. These can also become meteorites."

"I am so confused," says Lukas. "Asteroids, meteoroids, meteors, meteorites, comets! How can you possibly tell the difference?"

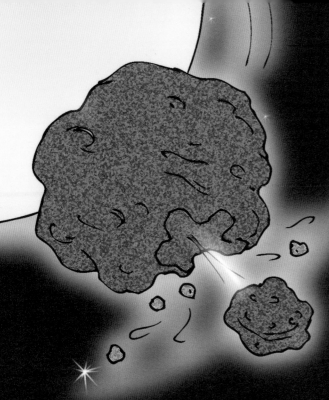

Dr. Dee Dee recites a cheerful chant
to help Lukas remember.

An *asteroid* is a great big rock,
That revolves around the sun,
Sometimes little pieces break off,
Those are *meteoroids* having fun.

When, in a quick flash,
One streaks across the sky,
It's called a *meteor* or *shooting star*,
Have you ever seen one go by?

When a *meteoroid* collides with Earth,
A loud BOOM we may hear.
It may sometimes leave a crater,
That's a *meteorite* causing fear!

"Aha! I get it!" exclaims Lukas. "But what is a comet?"

Kyle rolls his eyes up to the sky. "Lukas, no more questions,"
he begs with a tired sigh.

"Let's get the team ready," Dr. Dee Dee says urgently. "We must help." She activates the alert button on Wyndee Watch and zips towards her workroom.

NOT EVEN THE SKY IS THE LIMIT!

Freeda the Flying Ambulance is ready and waiting.

"Are all the instruments ready?" Dr. Dee Dee asks Marky Medicine Bag.

"They are clean, sharp, and ready for action, Dr. Dee Dee!" says Marky with gusto.

"Team, fasten your seatbelts. Freeda, set GPS for the meteorite collision site in Earth's Northern Hemisphere," directs Dr. Dee Dee.

Freeda begins her descent and Lukas peers out of the window. "Where are we?" he asks.

Dr. Dee Dee looks out. "Oh my!" she says. "The GPS must have become excited when she heard 'meteorite site' and has brought us to the oldest and largest visible, impact crater in the world. We are at Vredefort Dome in South Africa which formed when a meteorite collided with Earth two billion years ago."

"Two billion years ago!" Marky Medicine Bag says in amazement. "How old is Earth?"

"4.5 billion years old!" Dr. Dee Dee replies with glee.

"Wow! Look at those rock formations," exclaims Lukas. "Can we stop for a moment?"

"Excuse me, Mister Distraction! Let me remind you that we are on a mission," admonishes Kyle.

Dr. Dee Dee responds patiently. "I love these formations, Lukas."

"I've never seen such an odd shape," comments Lukas.

"These formations resulted when the intense heat released from the meteorite collision melted the rocks and bent them into the shape of an upside down bowl," explains Dr. Dee Dee. "We can return at another time."

"Freeda, we are clearly NOT in the Earth's Northern Hemisphere! Gordon, which country should we be going to?"

Gordon's sensitive ears hear Dr. Dee Dee's question and he pops onto the GPS screen. "This meteorite strike is in Russia," he says.

Freeda blasts off and after some time, lands with a resounding SPLASH. "Arriving in Russia, Dr. Dee Dee."

"Holymackarolee! What in the world!" exclaims Lukas.

"Unbelievable! I am getting seasick," complains Kyle as Freeda bobs up and down.

"Oh dear, the GPS is confused again," says Dr. Dee Dee. "We are at a meteorite site in Russia, but this collision occurred more than 100 years ago. This was the Tunguska meteorite."

"I don't see a crater," remarks Lukas.

"We are on Lake Cheko which is believed to be the crater."

"We don't know that for sure," says Kyle. "Scientists are still debating."

"You are correct, Kyle. There are several hypotheses on what happened here."
Dr. Dee Dee concurs.

"Freeda, reset GPS specifically for the 2013 Chelyabinsk meteorite collision," commands Dr. Dee Dee.

Freeda takes off again.

"*Hmmmmm*. How many meteorite craters are on Earth?" Marky wonders.

"We know of 130 craters," responds Dr. Dee Dee.

"My favorite crater is in Chixalaub, Mexico. That meteorite collision is believed to have caused the extinction of the dinosaurs. If I were there, I could have saved those dinosaurs."

"Are you serious, Dr. Dee Dee?" says Kyle in utter disbelief. "How could you have possibly saved the dinosaurs?"

"I am sure she would have found a way," says Marky confidently.

"Remember Kyle, NOT EVEN THE SKY IS THE LIMIT!" Dr. Dee Dee responds passionately.

BIG SONIC

"Approaching Chelyabinsk, Russia," announces Freeda. "Meteorite 2013."

"Great!" applauds Marky. "We can tell Astrid Asteroid that we have found her lost piece."

"Holymackarolee! Why is there so much broken glass?" questions Lukas.

"The meteorite created a SONIC BOOM when it entered the Earth's atmosphere, which shattered the glass on the buildings," replies Dr. Dee Dee.

BOOM!

"What! Meteorites make sounds?" asks Lukas with an incredulous gasp.

"Yes, they do!" grins Dr. Dee Dee. "When an object travels through the air, it creates a series of pressure waves in front and behind that travel at the speed of sound."

"The meteorite travels faster than the speed of sound so waves cannot get out of the way and are pushed together until they build up to form one huge sound wave which is powerful enough to break glass."

"Where is the meteorite?" queries Marky in a concerned voice.

Dr. Dee Dee Dynamo responds gently, "Matty Meteorite has broken into lots of little pieces. Come on, we have a lot of work to do."

"Marky, convert Freeda into a mini operating suite and prepare surgical tables," Dr. Dee Dee instructs.

"Kyle, line up the injured, bring them into Freeda, and position them on the stretchers."

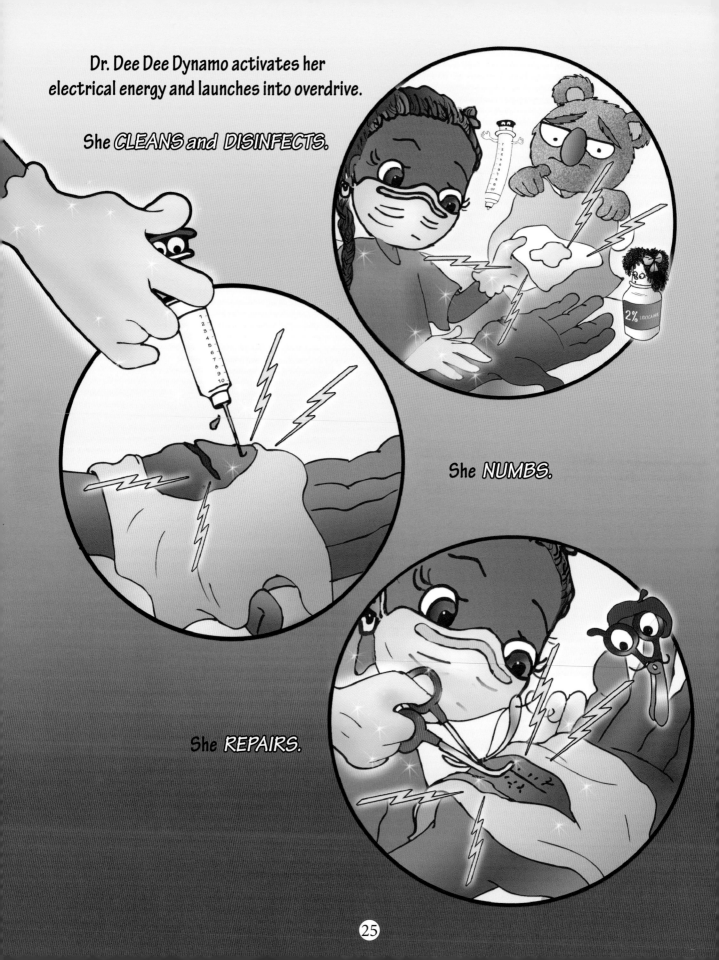

Sew, tie, cut....
Sew, tie, cut....
Sew, tie, cut....

Sew, tie, cut....
Sew, tie, cut....
Sew, tie, cut....

WAHOO! WAHOO! WAHOO!

Kyle covers his ears. "Noooooooooooooo!" he cries.

Gordon pops onto the GPS screen. "Matty Meteorite wants to be put back together."

"Absolutely not!" bellows Kyle. "He has caused too much destruction."

Gordon reasons, "He's really sorry and Astrid Asteroid is still sobbing."

"Okay, meteorite repair coming up!" declares Dr. Dee Dee.

Dr. Dee Dee Dynamo raises her arms, creates an intense electromagnetic field, and the meteorite pieces happily whizz toward her.

She grasps Nellie and Suzy once again
and Simon follows.

Sew, tie, cut.... Sew, tie, cut....
Sew, tie, cut....

They connect all the fragments until
Matty Meteorite is restored to one
gargantuan rock!

Lukas' eyes are wide with wonder.
"Stellar job, Dr. Dee Dee!"

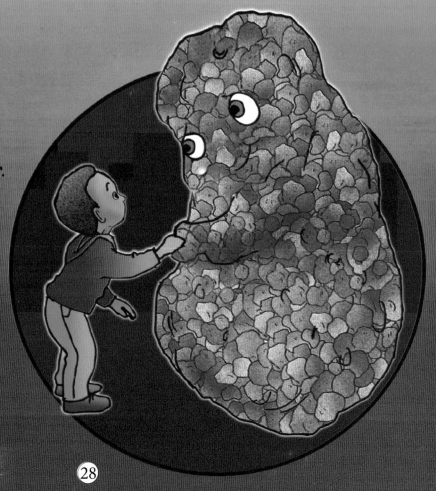

"Our work is not done," says Dr. Dee Dee. "We need to reunite Astrid Asteroid with her meteorite."

"Why?" mutters Kyle. "Just so he can do this all over again?"

"Oh Kyle, Matty Meteorite did not do this deliberately," responds Dr. Dee Dee. "This was an act of nature."

"Freeda, activate TURBO mode," commands Dr. Dee Dee Dynamo.
She focuses her electrical energy at Matty Meteorite and creates a
traction beam that attaches him to the flying ambulance.

Freeda guns her engines and blasts off into space towards the
anxiously waiting Astrid Asteroid.

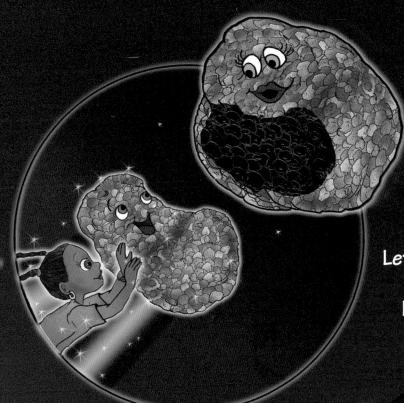

Dr. Dee Dee exits Freeda, keeping the beam focused on Matty Meteorite, and deftly fits him back where he belongs.

"Suzy, Nellie, and Simon. Let's secure Matty Meteorite so that he doesn't break off again," she says.

Sew, tie, cut....
Sew, tie, cut....
Sew, tie, cut....

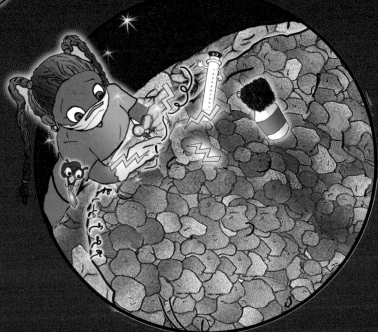

"Thank you for being so kind, Dr. Dee Dee Dynamo, SUPER SURGEON ON THE GO!" Matty Meteorite says gratefully.

"Thank you *soooooo* much for bringing Matty back," gushes Astrid Asteroid.

"You are both welcome!" Dr. Dee Dee says graciously.

Kyle grumbles, "Enough chit chat. I have been away from my leaves all day and I am hungry, tired, and grumpy."

"You are always hungry, tired, and GRUMPY!" teases Lukas.

"Congratulations team! EXCELLENT work!"
Dr. Dee Dee says with jubilation.

"MISSION COMPLETED!"

"LET'S GO HOME!"

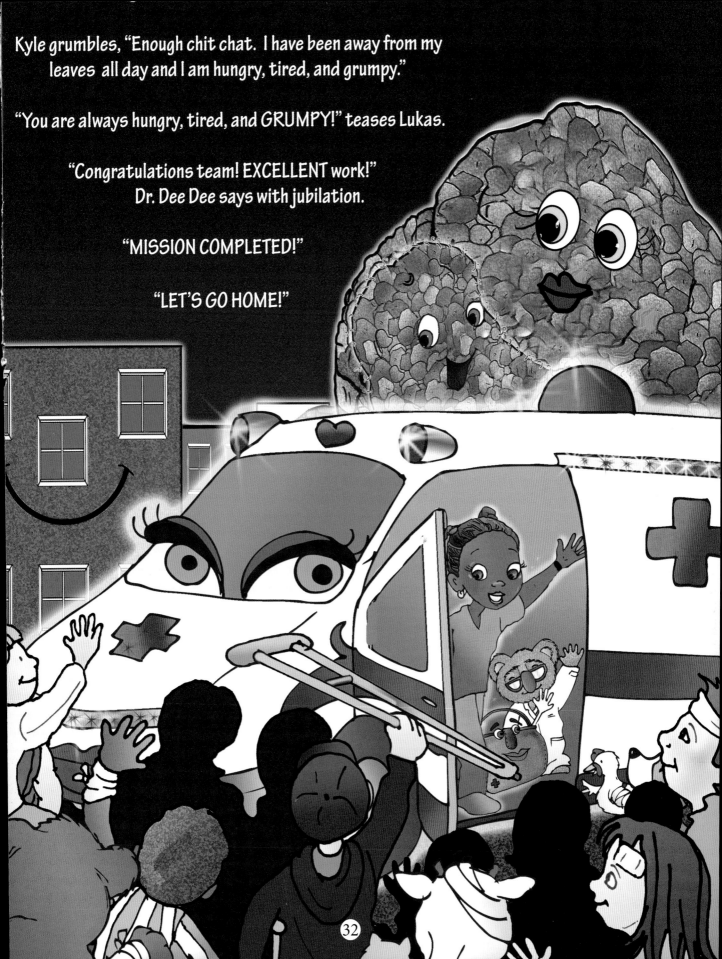

GLOSSARY

Chelyabinsk: City in the Ural region of Russia, near the border of Europe and Asia. It is the site of a meteorite impact in February 2013 and the only meteorite impact confirmed to have caused injuries.

Comet: Asteroid-like object covered with ice and dust. As it moves near the Sun, a vapor tail of dust and gas forms and streams after it.

Crater: Deep depression in the Earth's surface.

Extinction: Has ended or died out.

Lake Cheko: Small fresh water lake in Siberia, which may be the impact crater for the Tunguska meteorite.

Meteor: A chunk of interplanetary debris that burns up as it passes through Earth's atmosphere creating a flash of light that we can see in the night sky.

Meteorite: A mass of stone or metal that has fallen to Earth's surface from outer space.

Meteoroid: A solid body moving in space, smaller than asteroids.

Northern Hemisphere: The half of the Earth that is north of the equator.

Sonic: Speed that is the same as the speed of sound in air.

Sound waves: Exist as variations of pressure in air. They are created by vibration of an object, which causes the air around it to vibrate. The vibrating air causes the human eardrum to vibrate which the brain interprets as sound.

Tunguska event: Major explosion that occurred over the Tunguska region in Siberia on June 30, 1908, causing hundreds of miles of destruction and thought to be related to the impact of a cosmic body with Earth. In May 2013, scientists announced the discovery of rocks that provide evidence that a meteorite caused the damage.

Vredefort Dome: Vredefort crater is the largest meteorite crater on Earth. It measures more than 300 km across and is located in the Free State Province of South Africa. It is named after the town Vredefort, which means "Peace" or "Tranquil Fort" in Afrikaans. The dome is the central part of the crater. Much of the original crater has eroded.

LEARNING WORDS

Admonish: warn, scold in good-willed manner

Applaud: to show approval or praise by clapping

Concur: agree

Debate: discussion where opposing views are put forward

Deft: quick and skillful

Gasp: inhale suddenly with mouth open, in astonishment

Glee/ Gusto: enjoyment, delight, pleasure

Haughtily: superior tone, full of pride

Hypothesis: a theory, concept not yet proven

Incredulous: expressing disbelief

Gargantuan: giant, massive, towering

Miffed: annoyed, irritable

Module: independent units that can be part of a whole

Nudge: a light touch or push

Placid: calm, quiet, peaceful

Query: ask, question

Resounding: huge, ringing, loud enough to echo

Sarcastic: cutting remark

Skeptical: not easily convinced, having doubts

Startle: surprise suddenly, to give someone a fright

Stellar: outstanding

Mommy Dynamo's Discovery Questions

1. a. What is an asteroid?
   b. Write the sentences that gave you clues for your definition.

2. List 2 ways in which asteroids are similar to planets.

3. What evidence do scientists use to indicate that a meteorite crashed into the Earth?

4. Describe and explain the effects caused by meteorites crashing into Earth's surface.

5. Give at least 2 reasons why Dr. Dee Dee said, "Freeda, we are clearly not in Earth's Northern Hemisphere", when the team arrived at Vredefort Dome in South Africa.

6. Explain why the GPS became confused before it finally located the meteorite 2013 site in Chelyabinsk, Russia.

7. How were the people and community of Chelyabinsk affected by the meteorite? How did most of the injuries occur? How were Dr. Dee Dee and her team helpful?

8. How are sound waves generated?

9. How is a sonic boom formed? Find other examples where sonic booms are formed.

10. With what significant event is the crater in Chixalaub, Mexico, associated?

11. Make up your own chant to describe the differences between asteroids, meteoroids, meteorites, and meteors.